Assander

The White Hare of Hartland

The first story of the White Hare of Hartland

by Clive Brocklehurst

A catalogue record for this book is available
from the British Library

ISBN: 978-0-9573669-0-9

Published by White Hare
67 The Square Hartland Bideford Devon EX39 6BL
2012

www.whitehare.co.uk
www.clivebrocklehurst.com

Chapter One

1868

On yonder hill there sits a hare,
full of sorry grief and care...

The first words of a traditional Irish folk song. Some of these songs speak of the hare from the animal's point of view. Unusual as they date from a time of hunting, but in being hunted primarily for sport there is empathy. Something about the hare resonates throughout history in countless cultures from ancient to modern; it is a symbol of life and renewal *then and now*.

~~~

Assander sat on his powerful haunches and sniffed the chilled early morning air of the plains of Southern Ireland, lush green and lit by the pale morning sunrise. His nostril slits twitched above the split lip for which his kind is known.

Hares are solitary creatures save for the spectacle of March mornings when they gather to find a mate. No such gathering for this hare. The others had shed their winter coats of white but not so Assander, his had stayed, whiter than ever.

His glassy blue eyes gazed emptily, loneliness ached in his core.

Animals don't speak to each other as humankind does. They communicate and understand each other, frankly and clearly, through gesture, movement and through their minds' connection, of knowledge and image, a gift now lost to most humans as we fill our mind with noise and chatter. Having no language, animals deal in the now, the fact, be that waking or dreamtime. No imagined stories ringing in their heads, just the truth of *then and now*.

If you have ever woken a sleeping pet from a dream in which they show signs of distress or movement, you will have seen that on opening their eyes they know straightway where they are. No drowsy human confusion of uncertainty of place between dream and reality. They wake, they are here *now*, the dream was *then*, maybe a moment ago, maybe a lifetime, not forgotten just *then*, now is *now*.

And in the now Assander was alone and bitter. Cast out by the other hares, he could not belong, he was different and that suits no group. He was risk.

In the lush green grass of the slopes above Kinsale he was a beacon that the others knew would attract the huntsmen. He was too much of a prize. No mate would want him for fear of the leverets being like him.

Chapter 2

For a brief time then he had been happy. In the comfort of his mother's love he was cared for. As was the way of their kind she had given him his birth name; *Assander*. It echoed through his head, and she used it as she brought him up and taught him the ways of the hare. It referred to being a gift from the great hare spirit. When they had gathered with the others after his first winter, at his first spring ring, the elders had communicated that his colour meant that it was more likely the Great Spirit would be taking this gift back sooner than normal.

He could not hide now nature had removed its winter mantle of white snows and frosts.

The seniors of the ring soon made it clear he could not stay and he was to be chased away by the young bucks. Already heady with the prospect of mating and a future of note within the valleys, they wasted no time using their youthful strength to compete in persecuting the outcaste, the one different from their birth group.

Playful boxing turned to meaningful tearing and biting as they set upon him.

Freak...outcast...go...go...freak...ghost....go meet the spirit...you're not wanted here...you draw attention we do not want...you show up too much....there is something wrong with you....hares do not look this way in the warm days ...go freak....go

As his white body began to turn pink and then red with the beating and biting, he struggled to free himself from the circle of bucks taking their pleasure in attacking him. He broke free and for a moment saw his mother, a deep, deep sadness in her eyes, but now is now and this year's child becomes the offspring of then and she turned away and their connection was gone.

Assander ran and ran.

~~~

And now he sat some time later on this hillside. His bodily wounds had soon healed, he was young and healthy. But the cuts to his soul were deeper than the physical harm. If he did not belong in this ring then he knew no other would accept him. His mother had told him that none here had seen a hare of his kind but the elders knew that there had been white hares deep in the mists of then. But he was here now and hares were brown and there were none of his kind. And he could not live here.

Curse them all, he would find a place to live where he was accepted for what he was, not rejected through an accident of kind. Somewhere there would be others who would understand and accept him for what he was, whatever that may be. He would find his purpose and his home.

And as home was not here he would run, and with that he broke into the astonishing run of the hare. Designed for speed he loved to run. As he glided over the long grass he felt the wet of the morning dew on his underside. He darted sideways back and forth practising the trademark turns that had given rise to human legends of the hare appearing and disappearing. These skills placed them kin with the witches and spirits of nature that cannot be explained by mankind's ordinary experience.

For him to run was magic enough. He felt the energy course through his muscles, sinews and bones and his spirits lifted. The heads of the meadow plants blurred and sped by, early pollen bursting from grass heads as he brushed against them. The sun beating down casting shadows between the leaves that flickered and flashed like some entrancing light show.

This wondrous ability to run and the dexterity of their turns has placed the hare in the myths of many cultures. Unfortunately, it has also made them good sport for huntsmen.

Chapter 3

"Hunter?" shouted the taller man. No one in the bar turned or acknowledged the call. You can walk into some country pubs and it all goes silent and the regulars stare at you. Here they were totally ignored. The two stood there in their tweed breaches. They glanced at each other and started feeling rather foolish, more used to reaction and attention.

"Richard Hunter?" tried the shorter one, suddenly self-conscious of his hard English tone amidst the gentle background drone of the lilting Southern Irish voices frequenting the bar.

"Would you be keeping it down there" said a cloth capped, seated man. He was hunched with others around a table, monochrome patterned with dominoes and glasses of stout "there's important concentration being had here"

"We are looking for Richard Hunter" insisted Taller, red triangles appearing on his cheeks and a slight shake becoming visible around his jaw line "and we have good money to make our acquaintance worthwhile"

"Now why didn't you be saying that before" came a voice from the back of the bar, and as if a conductor had lowered his baton, a chorus of "I'm Richard Hunter", like a Celtic call and response song started immediately as ruddy face, upon chiselled jawbones, upon deep set eyes turned to acknowledge the two gents.

"Great..." sighed Shorter and stared despairingly at Taller, "you have a way with people"

"It's the only language they understand" snapped Taller under his breath.

The chorus died down at the scraping of a wooden chair on flagstone. One man eased himself to his feet and grasping a twisted blackthorn walking stick limped heavily towards them.

"Richard Hunter?" asked Shorter too eagerly.

"Shut up and get outside", snarled Hunter.

They blinked into the May noon sunshine and Hunter indicated a bench for them to sit at.

"We arrived last evening from Cork" started Taller "we have our prize greyhounds in the car, ready for hare coursing and we understand you're the man to help"

"I've seen the car" drawled Hunter. He was broad faced with blue eyes and dark curly hair "...it's very...shiny" he said as if the words tasted sour.

Shorter continued "You've heard of the white hare I'm sure... that's the one we want" nodding as he spoke.

"Hmm... I don't do hares. Not much of a hunter with this leg" grunted Hunter.

"Richaaard", said Taller ingratiatingly "...I may call you Richard?"

"Hunter will be fine" seethed Hunter through his teeth.

Shorter chipped in quickly "Mr Hunter, we know you are the man for hares and you know where to find them, your reputation runs far and wide. And now there is this white hare, you are the one to contact. We are used to the best and that is you"

"Not interested, hares are bad luck, that's how I got this leg" Hunter spat on the floor beside him.

"Oh don't start with myths and superstition. Hares are good sport and that is what we are here for" cheered Taller.

"Well I thought that once" mumbled Hunter.

Silence came between them. Shorter tried a gentler approach.

"I'm sorry to hear of your accident. We had no idea. Was it during a hunt?"

"Sort of" started Hunter seriously "It was my fault; too confident, arrogant. You probably know the feeling" He looked piercingly at taller, who shifted a bit on the creaking bench "I thought it would be fun to upset the coven with me dogs"

"Oh not witches, puh-lease..." chortled Taller

"Shut up" said Shorter exasperated. They were obviously getting somewhere, at least Hunter was talking. "Do go on Mr Hunter"

"Seemed fun to frighten a few wittering women" continued Hunter "I saw them dancing around and set the dogs on them. You never heard such screeches and damnations as uttered by them; sure 'twas like the banshees was let loose. I laughed and laughed but one caught my eye and that was when I felt the cold come into me..." he faltered and fell silent.

The two gents stared at each other not knowing if to speak would be inappropriate.

"Anyway..." Hunter started again softly coming out of his reverie "no sooner had things calmed down than out shot a hare from a side hedge and the dogs was off. Like something possessed they were away. I called and called but there was no having them back, they were on the chase and that was it. I ran and ran after them to keep tracks. The land became wilder, the soil heavier and before I knew it I fell, cracked me head and was out. When I awoke the dogs were with me but me leg was done for. I knew it. The pain was unlike anything I've had before. And mind in my game you get ... got ... your proper share of injury and harm. Get as good as you give perhaps. That was three year ago."

"So you're a fit chap", encouraged Shorter, "surely you mended"

"Not when you've been chasing a witch. That hare was not natural. They'd never come out when dogs are there, not choose to be coursed. It's known the witch and the hare can be as one. I seen them before, the enchanted ones, you can chase 'em, shoot 'em, try and trap 'em but they'll be no havin' them. And that fall, I'm more sure footed than that...at least I was... it never mended. The Doc would have no truck with my stories of witches and tried all things but still the pain grew. Eventually he had to admit it must be a cancer. He's known it in others. Right in your very bone marrow, growing, sappin', leachin' your life away, set off by a fall, but I knew 'twas the hare that cursed me for messing with the witches..."

"Well there you are then man" butted in Taller in his blustering way, warming to the possibility

14

of supernatural influence on Hunter to achieve, satisfying his bloodlust sport "...this is ideal revenge. Help us get the white hare and you'll have taken a rarity that'll go a way towards paying back for your misfortune. You never know, the forces of darkness might be that impressed as to let your leg get better" he chuckled, pleased at his insight.

"No" said Hunter, but not as definitely as he might have done. Shorter sensed a chink in the armour of denial.

"Still must be hard to make ends meet when you've had to give up your trade, your skill" said Shorter. Hunter was staring at the table deep in thought; Shorter looked at Taller out of the corner of his eye.

Taller got the drift "Perhaps this might help ease the pain" and landed a hefty wad of dog-eared notes on the table in front of Hunter. "We do have the best dogs you can buy and are prepared to pay well for our sport. Slasher and Ringwood are from the finest Irish greyhound coursing lines and we like nothing better than to test them. Come on, one more time Hunter, for old times' sake and revenge, eh?"

They talked for a while yet and soon drinks were bought and conversation of fine hunts gone by flowed, and before the afternoon was out Hunter had agreed to one more hunt, for the White Hare.

"We'll see you on the plains, 8 o'clock tomorrow morning" Shorter cried from the car.

They drove off horn hooting, dogs barking and Taller driving none too cautiously, fuelled by the afternoons talk, glasses of stout and some celebratory whisky chasers. Hunter was regretting already.

Chapter 4

It was still cold in the mornings and Assander's small breath showed in the crisp air as he surveyed the day. Another day alone of course but he felt the sun would shine and it could be a good day. He loped across the farm track in the awkward movement of his kind when moving slowly, and into the pastures of the plains. There was plenty of room for him to not bother the other hares; he might even loosen up with a run. For now as the sun glinted over the hills he stretched first upwards, straining his head up then downwards opening his chest in the salute to the sun his mother had taught him.

Time to head for the valley as had become his regular haunt in past weeks. There was water and lush spring grass aplenty. There were those that said he could eat as much as any sheep but thankfully most country folk know that hares and man can co-exist without harm to each other's welfare and live in the balance the universe condones. Little did he know what awaited him at his now regular haunt and the journey it would lead to for our lost Assander.

They had parked the car in a small copse of trees and unloaded Slasher and Ringwood, the dogs eager but well behaved, their deep chests beginning to heave in expectation. Their tight lips were drawn back over their sharp white fangs, their slim pointed noses tested the air for their quarry, tongues draped from the sides of their mouths.

Hunter had sent the gents up to the top of the slope as he crept along the hedgerow. He knew from local talk that the white hare had been seen regularly in this little valley. Since he had stopped organising coursing regularly the village had slipped out of its hunting ways and the animals, a new generation each year, were unaware of humans as predators and had become increasingly complacent in their presence.

He spotted the white hare, difficult not to thought Hunter, not the camouflage for these parts.

"Freak" he thought. This would be sweet revenge for the life he now had. After the dogs had got him he would take the long white ears to the crones and see what they would think of that.

The time had come; Hunter could see the gents with the dogs pulling at their leads. He signalled with his hand and bellowed "HARK-AWAY!!!" His voice echoed around the valley like a gunshot, making even the dog owners jump.

His voice was like thunder to Assander. With the echoes it seemed to come from all directions. He froze, not certain what was happening, and then all his instincts were on fire as he saw Slasher and Ringwood charging down the hill, their backbones arching back and forth as they effortlessly slipped into overdrive in their quest for flesh, their mouths agape, saliva flecking the air around their bobbing heads.

He leapt and ran using all his breeding, all his history, all the ancestry that had lead him to be able, right back to the Great Hare. But he was not considering lineage, he knew only that this was life or death.

He turned, ninety degrees as only his kind can, as if to disappear, line of sight and energy continue in the first direction, whilst the hare goes sideways in another. The dogs knew this, aside from experience, their bloodlines meant they had an instinct in their very souls and their bodies were made for lithe movement speed and rapid turns. They were behind him again.

Shorter and Taller were jumping with glee at the sight of their pedigree greyhounds at full speed in the fine morning air.

"Six turns, and the game is mine" shouted Taller to Shorter and they both stared down like two over excited youngsters at the chase, blood pumping in their veins and sick exhilaration striking through their bodies.

Hunter had struggled back up the slope and came to stand between the gents. The joy of the hunt he used to feel seemed tarnished now and as he watched the white hare leap and bound ahead of the dogs his leg ached. He knew he had made the most terrible error in bringing this blood thirsty crew to the valley. Pieces of silver he thought, you have sold your soul for pieces of silver and now this fine creature will be slaughtered for sport, and nothing else.

The words of the old folk song rang in his head

And tis now I must die

Yet I know not the crime

To the value of sixpence

I ne'er harmed mankind

"Five turns!" screeched Taller "one more and the game is mine!" He slapped Hunter roughly on the shoulder "A bonus for you too my man!"

Assander could not shake the dogs. He felt them nearing, could hear their breathing, could almost feel the heat of their bodies. His wide vision splay just caught each of them with their slavering mouths edged with froth, their wild eyes, demented in their quest for his blood. He was now running straight up the hill in the hope that the dogs might be slowed by the slope.

Another verse echoed in Hunter's mind

You can seek other pastimes

And drink hell's galore

On the plains of Kilgrain

You will hunt me no more

"He's coming straight towards us" cried Shorter "No chance of a turn, the valley narrows too much"

"Then I'll finish him anyway" murmured Taller through gritted teeth and raised the barrel of his shotgun.

"Mind the dogs" cried Shorter

"Don't worry, I'm a better shot than that you fool" sneered Taller

Assander's plan was working; he had lead the dogs a merry dance through the five turns and now the hillside was beginning to take its toll. Town dogs, no matter how good a pedigree, could not compete with a truly wild animal's fitness. He felt he could make it. The top of the hill was in sight with its tree cover and hedges.

But what was that he could see? MEN, three of them in a row and the one on the right seemed to be holding something to his shoulder.

Hunter saw the white hare coming towards him and he felt to his very core that its death would be more of a curse than any disruption of a coven. For the first time in his hunter's life he felt for the animal. This beautiful creature, perfectly balanced in its running, magical in its ability to turn and mis-foot the most skilled dog. This one was more special, this one was white, pure in form, unique amongst so many of its kind, and its death at the hands of these two barbarians, with their money and privilege, was wrong, too much to bear.

He had never felt this way, his father had raised him as a hunter, his surname was 'hunter', and his father had named him Richard after so many folksongs about hunters. But the last lines of that song chimed in his mind

The hounds in full cry

Were bred to obey

It was you Richard Hunter

"HARKAWAY!" he thundered again. The dogs looked up, this was not the call when they were in the last moments before the kill, confusion streamed through their bodies and they faltered, slowing slightly.

Assander was running too fast to do anything but move faster at this thunderous sound even if it was towards the men.

"You idiot Hunter, what the hell are you doing? Go on Slasher, go on Ringwood!" Shorter's gentler nature was consumed by the heat of the chase and he glowered at Hunter with eyes burning with bloodlust "He may still turn!"

"If they don't get him I will" snarled Taller and nestled the stock of his gun into his shoulder, raising the barrels to take aim.

"NO" cried Hunter and lunged at Taller knocking him sideways, as the gun went off in the air. Assander reached the top with the dogs in pursuit running between the men as Shorter went to grab him. Then the dogs were upon all of them, failing to leap in the confusion. They ploughed into the men and arms and legs seemed to be everywhere; a maelstrom of overheated bodies, sweat and adrenaline.

As quickly as Assander had started he stopped dead. Seeing no escape at the top of the valley behind the men he turned to look at the pile of flailing limbs, struggling to right themselves.

Suddenly everything went silent and Assander found himself staring with his sky blue eyes into six human and four dogs' eyes, bodies knotted and piled together.

In the moment they moved Assander leapt higher than he had every done before and cleared the mess of men and dogs. Their eyes followed his progress over their heads seeing his pink underside sail over them and watching as he landed and ran down the valley.

"Get him Slasher, get him Ringwood" screamed Shorter in a high pitched wail, but their rapid scrapings for traction were in vain as Hunter's strong hands grasped a rear leg of each and they yelped in agony, torn in different directions.

"You madman!!" cried Taller as they watched Assander's near unbelievable speed as he moved effortlessly down the slope to cover.

"Go Assander go" whispered Hunter

"What did you say?" growled Taller

"I don't know" said Hunter honestly, shaking his head as if waking from a dream; for it is few men that learn an animal's true name. It is only when they offer great service that the spirits of nature allow those who have learned to talk the luxury of true knowledge, but it is only fleeting, never remembered and cannot be uttered again.

Richard Hunter knew he would now be the quarry and as Taller lunged forward with his fists clenched, without thinking, he raised to his feet and set off down the slope. It was only after a few strides he realised he was running, the pain in his leg was draining away with every long stride down the hill, he gasped, a grin broke across his face and he whooped at the top of his voice and flailed his arms as he ran. He felt again the freedom he had known as a child playing on the plains in younger years, knowing he had been freed from the curse by a deed of great fortune to the white hare, whose name he already could not remember. The spirits of nature had repaid him by giving him another chance; a chance to use his skill and knowledge of nature's ways to the benefit of animals and man alike and not just for sport and base gratification.

Revenge may be sweet, but it is a fleeting flavour, whilst the taste of forgiveness lingers on the palette and stays with you forever.

Chapter 5

Assander kept running until nightfall. He had kept heading south. Although he did not know his direction soon he would be at the coast. His little nostrils scented something different on the air. He had never smelt it before but he would soon come to know it only too well.

The land ran out and turned to water. His run had slowed to a loping canter as he made his way eastwards along the shore line. This was a river greater than he had ever seen before. There was no sign of the other side.

Dusk was falling fast as he found himself at the edge of an inlet, the sea lapping gently on the shore. He stopped and felt the air chill, damp as the sun dipped below the horizon. He looked at the calm rippling water in the last evening light and listened to the unfamiliar bird call coming

29

across the bay from an island. Woodland came down to the seashore nearby and he made his way in to look for shelter for the night.

Behind some low branches were piles of wooden boxes stacked roughly on top of each other. Many had their tops removed and had straw billowing out with the necks of bottles sticking through. He found one which smelt less to him than the others and climbed in to settle down in the warm interior turning round and round to make a bed for the night. He slept and was once again on the plains with his mother, leaping and teasing her as they made their way across each meadow.

Assander didn't know it but he had reached Kinsale Bay. Although the export and import of alcohol from Ireland to the mainland had long been legalised it was still a centre for smuggling and he was asleep in the latest shipment.

~~~

"Just hurry up will you, we've got loads to do, the boat'll be here any time" a first broad Irish voice broke the peaceful dusk in a stage whisper.

"I'm comin' as fast as I can carryin' this lot; will you give me a break now" came a second voice thick with lilting accent.

The two men lurched through the darkness towards the shoreline, the second tripping and cursing as he went, lumbering along with a wooden box held between his arms.

"Put the lids on you lazy get and let's put 'em out by the shore" snapped the first.

"What did your last slave die of then?" grizzled the second.

The lids were wedged onto the few opened wooden boxes, trapping Assander inside his sleeping place. The next thing he felt was the box being lifted up and wielded roughly through the air.

"Stack 'em there, and be quiet you toad. I'll light the lantern and give the signal" ordered First.

As the boxes were piled up by the second man to a constant commentary of hushed groans and complaints, the first man fiddled with the lantern and then waved it at the bay. After a minute a similar light glinted back from the island.

"They should be here in a few minutes. It's a good night for a crossing" whispered First to a rather less interested Second.

True to prediction within a few minutes a small clinker built sail boat came into view being rowed across the harbour by two men. The only sound was the cutting of the bow through the sea and the drip of water from their oars as they raised them with skill that only comes from experience, and then silently carving them into the surface to give them their motion.

These were professionals at being invisible. Men who spent their lives in the shadows, who drank hunched at corner tables in the bars of Kinsale, and who smoked homemade roll ups curled into the palms of their large calloused hands. They did not want and did not like to be noticed.

Gruff greetings were exchanged and the boxes were loaded on board, the second of the men from the shore continuing to grumble but more quietly now that the other two were involved.

The boat was soon loaded and with the four on board the boat set off by oar power. It hugged the shoreline of the bay for a distance and then setting its sail as the gentle evening breeze filled the canvas the boat silently headed out to sea.

Once a fair distance off shore, the captain of the ship spoke "You are a moaner" he said to the grumbling Second from the shoreline and with that came a flurry of banter and jokes of the kind only heard in the back street bars amidst raucous and cackling laughter and the smashing of glasses.

Assander had never heard such noise and felt the motion of the boat from within his wooden casket. It made him feel sick. As the journey went on and the boat rose and fell he felt less ill and more aware of a crushing feeling within his skull.

At first it was like a pressure from the top of his head and then like a hand gripping the sides and pressing as if to crush. He had felt it before back on the plains before the weather turned.

Sharp needles of pain shot in from his temples and he began to writhe and squirm.

"Wassat?" said Second "There's something in that there box!"

"Yeah our next month's wages, eejit" retorted First

"No there's something alive in there, I tell ya!" insisted Second

"It's probably a rat" said the Captain

"I hate rats!" mumbled Second

"Pull the lid off and thwack it with a pin then, we don't want no stowaways" cackled the Captain, coughing the way only a smoker can.

The grumbler Second grabbed a stout wooden pin from the rigging settings and made to take the lid off the box.

"Ah, t'will be just like the ole 'splat the rat' contest at the fair. Mind not to waste any bottles tho!" encouraged First.

After some encouragement, using a steel pin, Second wrenched the lid off with a start. In an explosion of straw and white fur Assander leapt out like a jack-in-a-box onto the deck of the sailboat; the men stood around aghast.

"Well I'll be..." exclaimed the Captain before all started shouting and reaching for weapons.

Assander was totally disorientated by the freedom, the movement of the boat, the men roaring, the swiping of wood through the air and splintering on the box, and the pain in his head. He lurched and span round. He moved in between legs and along the edge of the boat, round the little cabin and back down the other side. Hands reached out towards him and boots slammed against the hull just behind him.

"What the hell is it?"cried one sailor as he fell uselessly against the side of the boat.

The men crashed over each other, a mess of heavy hands and clumsy boots. Assander was at one end of the boat and the men were now side by side and coming towards him. He cowered into the bow of the boat as the footsteps clumped towards him. The pain in his head became more and more and his body started to twitch and spasm.

"What's it doin?" asked First. The men stood and watched Assander's white body flailing in the corner, legs flicking out and backbone arching.

"I think it's sick like? Maybe it's got rabies? Watch out it might attack" panicked Second

"Rabies? Rabies!?" growled the Captain "It's a rabbit!!"

In the pandemonium the men had not noticed the oppressive air that had surrounded the boat and the wind dropping. As the men stood and watched the animal there was a slow distant rumble of thunder.

"Oh no!" said the Captain spinning round to see the towering black clouds above them "Please not a storm"

And with that a gust of wind hit the boat, the sail snapped full of wind and the whole vessel lurched to the side, throwing them all to the deck and against the side.

"Quick lower the sail!!" shouted the Captain as hands reached for ropes.

There was a flash of lightening and then a massive clap of thunder, heralding the arrival of the storm. Wind tossed the boat, waves lashed and then the rain came. Assander's head cleared at the first clap of thunder and he scurried under a nearby bench seat. The men were running back and forth lowering sail, altering rigging and securing ropes, tying down what they could.

The little smugglers' boat was no match for a storm like this, it drove them on towards their destination but they had no control. It felt to the captain like riding a drunken train heading towards an abyss with no brakes. He knew the coast up the Bristol Channel and if the wind continued to blow them south they would meet their fate on the rocky shoreline. The stories from his seafaring childhood and onwards poured into his head; of the Cornish and North Devon Coast and their appetite for ships and the men of the sea. He knew only too well how the steep cliffs fall away so abruptly to lines of jagged strata lying at right angles to the shoreline and stretching out one after the other. These rocks are like the teeth of saws ready to rip through the hulls of sea craft much greater than this little boat.

They moved on too swiftly, driven by the storm south eastwards, to the captain's dismay despite his efforts at the tiller. Assander huddled on under the benchseat protected a little from the waves breaking over the side. The crew had stopped worrying about intruders and taken to holding on to whatever they could to keep themselves safe, oblivious to whatever rats or rabbits might be riding the journey with them and more interested in whether they would be making landfall or meeting their maker.

As the rain wrapped around his face, the captain could see the beam from the lighthouse at Hartland Point and he knew from the way the storm was taking them that his boat was to be another name carved on the wall of the tavern at Hartland Quay, destined to become part of the stories of wrecks.

The locals would be very interested in this cargo he thought, and for a moment the vision of the white creature writhing and fitting before the storm came into his head and he wondered had the animal brought a curse upon his vessel?

Had his writhing brought the storm as if from nowhere?

Then the sea hurled another wave into his face like one last mocking flick of a gauntlet. He felt the first grind of wood on rock from beneath his feet and he was back to the reality of now, and the battle to survive.

Chapter 6

The night had been a wild one. Despite being nestled in a valley the cottage could suffer the brunt of a storm when the wind was coming in off the sea. More than by the storm Boy had been disturbed by the wreckers calling for his father; 'Wreckers' Rights' they call it. When a ship was wrecked it was all hands to the seashore or even better the wreck if it was accessible. Often captains would comment that it seemed as fast as they worked to get their crew off the ship, there were more people boarding as leaving.

The folk songs call them looters, pirates, thieves, but it was the way of life and Boy's dad's salvage of lost items and cargo, from the ships that regularly found themselves on the rocks off Hartland Peninsula, supplemented their subsistence existence. Their only income was from farming a few sheep on the cliff tops on borrowed land between the Quay and Point.

But it was morning and the sea was quiet. The house too was quiet. It was only him and his father. He could just remember his mother but she died a long time ago in his mind. His dad was either still out picking up debris or flat out on the floor at the tavern at the quay, having spent money on too much beer, the money yet to be raised from selling the loot.

Boy pulled on his old shirt and patched trousers over the underclothes in which he slept and went downstairs. His room was in the eaves but then so was the whole upper floor of the house. These days the roof's ridge dipped so much the rooms were getting smaller as he was getting bigger.

His father would joke that the wavy roofline matched the sea it looked out onto. But for their situation, they were lucky that the landlord was charitable in letting them live for little or no rent; allowing them to keep the few sheep. His mother had worked at the big farmhouse and his father, although not a craftsman, could wield a saw and hammer to help with odd jobs and fencing.

There was milk in the pantry so he gulped down a cupful and wiped his white moustache off on his cuff as usual. With no one around he figured he might as well wander down to the shore. Their little cottage was tucked at the bottom of one of the many valleys that lead down to the rugged shore of the peninsula.

The sun was on his back as he looked out to sea to Lundy Island. With mist laying around its base it looked magical, like it could be Avalon or another such mythical homeland. At the shore the tide was out but there was no great expanse of sandy beach here, mostly large rounded stones lying between the razor-edged vertical sheets of rock that jutted out like all along the coastline making it so treacherous for shipping. It meant the beach was virtually private, known as a secret beach, as, apart from a few low tides, the sand was seldom seen.

He loved it on the shore. As the cliffs rose up behind him the one on his left, as he clambered towards the sea, soared up in a curve that looked like the waves it so often faced, defiantly curving in mirror form to the very force that had helped shape its form.

The rocks were so many different shades of grey, run through with crisscrossing lines of white quartz and punctuated here and there with the ochres and oranges of mineral deposits. They shone when wet and often he had thought they could be gold glinting in the sun but in the heat of the day as the rocks dried the gold turned to ferrous ores; rich pickings elsewhere down the southwest coast, but not here, and certainly not for Boy.

There were bits of timber and wooden packing cases washed up from the wreck last night. More out of a youthful hope for treasure than his bloodline's scavenging nature he thought he would pick his way along the shore and see what he could find.

A few bottles tainted with sea water, plenty of rope shreds from rigging, the odd battered cooking pot; all these were shattered or beaten beyond useful or gainful employment or sale; just a mess really. He looked out to sea again and casually threw a shard of timber across the water. It skipped a couple of times on the surface and then floated out to the sea from which it had come.

He noticed something dirty white over by one of the angled vertical shards of rock sticking out between all the rounded pebbles on the beach. At first he thought it might just be foam blown in with the storm but most of that had long since gone as the sea had calmed its roiling.

He went further to explore and could see or even feel that it was the body of an animal. Somehow when he came across a carcass it never failed to make him start. Often they would be gulls, occasionally a dolphin. This was not he could see it had four limbs; it sort of sagged, deflated across the rocks on which it lay.

It must be a lamb, he thought, they sometimes got blown off the cliffs. He hoped it wasn't one of theirs; they could not afford to lose any. He briefly thought of the banter amongst the fishermen and traders at Hartland Quay and busier Clovelly. The fishermen would sometimes pick up a drowned lamb in their nets. They reckoned the crews down the coast in Cornwall had netted a flock of sheep still

45

alive and joked that the Cornishmen had thought they were a new species; 'sheepfish'! He could hear their coarse raucous laughter as the story was told for the hundredth time in the bar; it was happy noise nevertheless, harmless banter to relieve the harshness of their existence.

As he neared the ragdoll like body he saw it was not a lamb, it had huge ears. It looked like a large rabbit but with longer legs and bigger ears. There were rabbits on the cliff tops but none were white and certainly none as big as this, it was like a small deer. The animal's pelt was stuck together and matted, with bits of twig and seaweed caught in it. He poked it with a stick; it was lifeless.

He levered its chest up with a piece of wood, its front legs and ears hung down like a puppet. It was heavy but he thought he could turn it over. He got it up onto its side. He could see its face now with a long, arch-topped nose leading down to its slit-nostrils and then split lip beneath, perfectly divided from nose to mouth. It had long whiskers and he reached forward with a twig in his other hand and gently flicked the fine white strands. Suddenly two sky blue eyes were staring directly at him, eyelids back pupils dilated, its gaze intent but empty.

Boy squealed and jumped backwards dropping his stick and falling with a thump onto his backside into a small rock pool. His legs draped over the front of the pool and looking a complete fool. He hauled himself up quickly and clumsily with his two arms. Despite being alone he still looked around awkwardly, acutely embarrassed by his feminine shriek and now by a wet backside as well. Forgetting himself and the animal for a moment he cussed and swore like his father could. He brushed himself off and tried to compose himself but then in sudden remembrance swung round to the body in a defensive stance.

The body was lifeless and drooping as before but he could see its chest moving. It was alive. Cautiously he edged forward taking the stick again and poked the side of the animal. Nothing, lifeless, it could be dead, but he knew it was just unconscious.

He decided he would take it back to the cottage. This was not an easy task as the dead weight of the animal was quite something for his stature.

The lengthy limbs and ears seemed to go in all different directions as he tried to pick it up. He struggled to control the limbs and comical ears as the neck flopped around. The body came to a compromising rest in his arms. With head, ears and front legs draped over his right arm and back legs and bottom over the left, he turned and struggled over the uneven terrain and up the steep cliff path back towards home.

He was now in silhouette, tottering up the beach like a warrior carrying his wounded colleague back from a battle ground. Slow progress but purposeful; he felt the warmth within the limp damp body and he could feel a heart beat faint but constant.

Chapter 7

Assander knew nothing of this. His eyes had not registered Boy in their momentary opening. In his mind he was running and playing with other hares so white they glowed. Happiness and acceptance coursed through him.

Colours, bright azure sky blues bursting through brilliant yellow greens, pastures so soft and lush, slopes so gently undulating, a breeze just perfect in your face and ears as you ran. First one was ahead, then he was, then two boxed playfully in front of him jousting and rising up until one fell joyfully right over backwards. Up the hill they ran, up, up and as they ran the brilliant sky blue that enveloped them turned deeper to cobalt and then the deep dark indigo of the night sky and they jostled and circled in the moonlight, whites, silvers, greys, they leapt and played with such abandon that their movements seemed to become more and more effortless, lighter and lighter ...and then they flew.

Upwards, over towering trees towards the moon; the brilliant, beautiful, gold and white moon. They circled, they soared.

And then Assander was aware of a beautiful woman's face, a slim neck, fine features and hair of ashen grey tumbling down. He knew who it was, all hares know, they are born with the knowledge that has come through the generations then and now. It is why they stare at the moon; to 'hear' her voice. This was the Goddess of the Moon, sometimes called Cynthia in human myth and legend.

No words were uttered; but understanding came.

Assander said Cynthia

I am your servant replied Assander

You are indeed; as all white hares are born to do my bidding so are you. You have an unusually pure and sensitive spirit Assander. I have work for you Cynthia spoke kindly.

I can only do as you ask said Assander bowing his head slightly but keeping her gaze

Her face was opposite him now and their noses nearly touched.

It is not your time to stay here again, now you have work to do in the world said Cynthia as softly as a breeze on a summer's eve.

Assander's demeanour weakened slightly, he had been so happy playing with the other hares, it was so beautiful here.

You have a gift Assander, one with which all hares are blessed but of which few make use. This gift is especially strong in you, and you must use this in the world. If you do not use it, it will die with you. You must leave that legacy before your duty is done and you can join me again for your next task continued Cynthia

What talent? asked Assander

You already know, but having been born from, and into the company of worldly hares it has not been nurtured. You will find out and know when you go back, and you must use it or like any unused gift from the universe if wasted it

will be lost and taken back and may take aeons to be found for use again explained Celia with a tone that could do nothing but reassure and convey a truth so pure that it could not be questioned.

I am your servant said Assander, he felt calm and satisfied. Hares were born for this, then and now, it was no chore it was what is meant to be.

Go now, finished Cynthia

And the colours gathered around him and the beautiful face began to fade as her words echoed in his mind, and the other white hares on the lush meadows stopped and looked on kindly as he began to withdraw through the colours, knowing they would see him again as if in an instant as the folds of time, space, light and shadow rippled between their gaze.

Chapter 8

Boy settled the body on some straw on the floor of the outhouse gathering more around the animal's outline. Feeling rather awkward, not being fully acquainted with the animal's kind, he tried arranging its head and ears to look comfortable. As he moved its legs into place he marvelled at the muscles and its physique. This was unlike any rabbit he had handled before.

From behind him came a scuffling, a kick and a trip, a shuffle and a belch. It was dad. The boy looked as his father peered around the door.

"What-ch ya doin' in here then son?" said the man quite softly "Sorry not to come home last night. It was a good wreck, plenty to be had; the lads have got a good haul, we should be made for a month or two off this one. I, er, stayed at the Quay... at the tavern..." the man shifted slightly, Boy knew from the fumes creeping round the door the form his father's sleep had taken; no doubt face down on a hard floor in the tavern's stables. He didn't mind, his dad was never nasty with the drink, just unreliable.

"You got something worthwhile then?" spoke the man encouragingly.

"A rabbit I think" Boy moved to one side to display the white outstretched body. He had cleaned it with some water and straw and it was nearly white as snow now.

The man leaned in a bit more as his eyes became accustomed to the darker interior.

"Phew that's some rabbit boy!" chuckled the father, "Naah, that's no rabbit that there is a hare, like you see further in land up round Stoke and over towards Woolsery way. Mind I never heard of a white one afore. Is it dead? They makes fine eatin'!"

"No, it's still alive" cut in Boy quickly "I was going to see if I can make it better; maybe train it or something?"

The father was kindly to his only son and kin, they did not have much, certainly no luxury of a pet. He supposed the boy could mess around with it for a while, it would either die or run off anyway.

"Up to you lad, luck has it that we won't be going hungry for a few weeks after last night's treasures. I'm just going to check on the sheep and then I said I'd meet the lads back at the bar to see how we divvy up the spoils.... I won't be back 'til late I, er, brought some cold meat and bread back from the pub kitchen, it's on the side in the pantry...you be good now and I'll see you on the moro".

"Alright Dad" said boy turning back to his patient and stroking the soft white fur of the animals neck "So you're a hare then?" he said to Assander.

The boy sat with the hare all evening and into the night finally falling asleep in the straw next to him.

As dawn broke the boy awakened, hearing the waves crashing below and the wind moaning around the door to the outhouse he knew it was not a fine day, no birds singing and no gentle light.

The hare was twitching, its limbs tensing, its eyes moving quickly back and forth beneath its eyelids. The boy was worried "Wake up" he said and laid his hand on the hare's chest. The hare convulsed like an electric shock and the boy swiftly withdrew his hand like it had been bitten. The body started to writhe and then unannounced a bolt of lightning split the sky with a sound that felt as if the whole world might have been split in two. Then immediately there was a massive clap of thunder.

The hare writhed violently and then stretched out rigid, all of its body taught until, when the roll of thunder had died down, he went limp. Was he dead? Boy lent forward ... the hare was still breathing, on his own pink cheeks he could feel its breath through the small slits of its nostrils.

He thought; he did not have the knowledge of caring for an animal like this and yet he felt drawn to look after him. He was beautiful and so white, like the waves of the sea that had brought him here.

A flash of inspiration came to him; the crone. She lived in a tiny stone hut up on the cliff tops above the valley. Few went near her save for when they had troubles that needed healing; a rash, a boil, a fever, a case of the gloom. Like all crones she knew things about the way plants affected the bodies of men and women. And even though most would not give her the decency of a nod if they passed her in the village they soon found themselves visiting when the need came; illness but particularly childbirth. She had no children of her own but then nobody could remember how she came to be in the area or what age she might be.

Boy fetched an old blanket from the cottage; not that there were any new ones. He slowly rolled the hare into the blanket, folded corner to corner and, as gently as he could, lifted the body; which was not very gentle at all. As the hare's head flopped in and out of the homemade papoose, he lifted the bundle over his shoulder and started to walk out of the outhouse with a slight totter reminiscent of his father's gait after an evening at the bar at the Quay. He started up the coast path over the cliffs one step at a time.

It was mid morning by the time he had gone up and down to the top. The farms always seemed closer than they really were when you looked across the cliffs; it's the valleys in between that catch you out his father would say. The boy's small form carrying his parcel on his back edged up each step methodically. With a pair of paws sticking straight out of one end and a large long pair of white ears flopping comically out of the other end of the bundle it was a funny and yet pathetic sight.

Finally he reached the top, panting furiously at the exertion, his cheeks crimsoned. Assander's limp body was still resting motionless in the blanket which he now laid down gently by him. He folded back the layers and sat down watching the hare's short shallow breathing. He hoped the old crone would or could help.

His eyes rose to the sea. He could hear waves crashing on the pebbled shore below. The sea breeze cooled his face and he smelt the fine tinge of brine on it. He thought of the days he had spent sitting on the beaches below perched on one of the myriad of large smooth pebbles, listening to the waves crashing and watching the sea foam burst up the cliff face and rise on

58

up in a swirling show like snowflakes spinning skywards.

He always felt at one with the sea. He loved to play in the waves and dreamt of being a fisherman. His father had brushed the idea aside when he had mentioned it, saying you do not want to risk your life on the waves; he had seen too many taken. Nevertheless the boy had a secret yearning ambition and he held it in his heart to pursue when he was a man.

For now though it was time to take his chances with the crone. He picked up Assander again and made his way unsteadily along the path to the little stone hut of the crone.

Chapter 9

It was a tiny building but then the crone was the smallest woman the boy had ever seen.

As he neared the hut with its stone walls and wood shingled roof, smoke was blowing out of the door; a strange smelling smoke, sweet, not like that of the tobacco smokers in the tavern. The crone was always gathering plants, leaves and barks from the cliff tops or in the deep wooded valleys that led to the sea.

He walked quietly towards the hut and jumped when a shout like a gunshot erupted from within.

"Who's there?" came the hard piercing voice. She couldn't have seen him yet, so how did she know he was there?

"What da ya want?" came a second barked phrase "youngsters like you only have mischief coming up around the crone, be off with you!"

"No, no please I have a sick animal. I have carried him all this way" said Boy

Still unseen by the boy the voice came "You're the lad from the valley ain't you? What you got? One of your dad's scabby lambs for me?" sniggered the crone.

"No, it's a hare" said Boy pleadingly. Then quietly, almost to himself he added "He came from the sea, he is beautiful. I can't get him to wake up"

"A hare you say? From the sea eh? Never heard of one of them before" there was a sing-song mocking tone in the quavering tones of the crone "Don't suppose you've got any money to pay for an old girl's skill then?"

"No" said the boy feeling he may have wasted his time. His weary arms let Assander slip to the ground from the blanket.

"Well I dare say you can owe me" said the crone's voice softening more "and will come up with something one day that you can repay me with". Her face appeared around the side of the door "well bring him here then".

The boy hesitated for a moment on seeing the wizened craggy face with its hook nose and whiskery chin curtained by long matted hair. But thinking of his purpose he checked his rude gaze, picked up Assander in his arms and carried him over to the crone. Laying him down in front of this little woman he explained how he had found the hare the night after the great storm. His voice petered out as he finished the explanation of climbing the coastal path to her door.

The crone seemed not to be listening but was looking intently at Assander. Her gnarled hands, yellowed from the sulphurous mixtures she concocted, hovered above the body, quivering and moving backwards and forwards

"He's a funny thing, never seen a pure white one. Heard of 'em. Many's a folks think they're mighty special and have stories and legends that go back to the start of time. That bloke from

Americay that stayed in the Abbey grounds t'other year told us his people believe the creator is a hare. Round here the witches have a liking to take their shape and taunt the hunters..." She too trailed off and closed her eyes, still holding her hands above the hare.

She spoke "He's full of the sea, damp to the core, it's got into his life's very energy and it's all his body can do to keep going. We'll have to give him something to tell his spirit it still has a body that it needs to come back to"

The boy hurriedly told the crone of the fit the hare had suffered during the thunder storm.

"I dare say, as he's all white, he's got a sensitive nature, often the way with the freak ones. You never had a headache when a storm approaches lad?" He thought and nodded yes he did feel odd on the days when storms were brewing but he had never thought anything of it. "There's some can have a savage reaction....'she trailed off again "his breathing's a-getting slower and thinner, he's not long for this life"

"But surely you can do something?" pleaded Boy

"We'll get some sea-wort tincture in him straight way and spike it with hawthorn and fire-berry juice" she said thinking and stroking her chin. The boy had only heard of hawthorn and blackthorn so was none the wiser. The crone turned went into the little hut and returned with a branch from which hung many small brown bottles of all shapes. They had greasy, dirty corks in their necks and rags tied round them with crude symbols written in charcoal on grubby paper labels. She balanced the branch on two 'Y' shaped pieces of wood stuck into the ground to the side of the hut. She sorted through them talking to herself, her fingers running over them, the bottles tinkling and chiming.

Having gathered what she needed and come back to Assander and Boy she settled down on her knees and closed her eyes and breathed deeply. Boy thought how for someone of such great age she neither wheezed nor coughed like all the other old people he knew. She poured tiny drops of liquid from three bottles into a

65

battered little tin ladle with a short twisted handle.

"Here you hold his head up so I can put some of this in his mouth" she instructed

The boy cupped the soft white head in his hands, the hares ears hung limply between the boy's wrists. The crone leant forward and poured a tiny amount of liquid between the hares split lip. "See that lip, there's many a story of how he got that, some say he was a dancing with the devil and held the dark one's very own fiddle string in his mouth for to save a maiden and that's how he got it cut like that"

The boy wasn't listening he was watching the hare's reaction; nothing.

The crone pursed her lips and seeing the boy's anxiety said "We may be wasting our time little 'un. He's so weak there's little or no flicker of his soul's fire left"

"There must be something else you can do" said the boy

The crone could be sympathetic despite her harsh tones. The mothers who needed help in birth were always struck by how kindly she was when they needed reassurance. She did not believe in wasting time on niceties but dealt with people as they needed. She had long since needed to ingratiate herself to people. You were not a healer without having a great sense of feeling.

She started "Ok lad I'm going to add some more of the fire-berry essence and some monk-worthy, it's a risk but it's our only hope and then I'm going to put my hands on him too and we must both tell his spirit his body is still here, it's like its forgotten it has a body 'cos its stopped using it. He is somewhere else at the moment but my heart says that he has to come back, I've known it many a time afore, I just feel nature has some purpose for him here"

The boy looked up at the crone's face. Her eyes were bright and for a moment she did not look so wrinkled and he thought he saw what she may have looked like once, maybe even she was beautiful then.

She mixed a new potion and once again they gently administered it. Then she laid her hands on the hare's chest and haunches, the white fur made her hands look even more yellow. The boy's young, pink hands held the hare's head and he concentrated as hard as he could on what the crone had said to ask.

The hare's breathing seemed softer than ever. The boy was sure they could bring him back, he did not know why but he too knew there was a reason for him to come back.

"Come on" he said in his head "come on"

The crone started to move back resigning herself to letting the animal go.

"No wait" said the boy desperately "just one more time, please". She liked the boy he had honesty in his soul. She leant forward and placed her hands again and closed her wrinkled eyes tightly. The lad did the same.

"Come on" he said in his head "come on" and then quietly under his breath, he knew not why, but he said "Come on Assander you're needed"

With that the hare's eyes opened and the sky blue pupils stared straight into the boy's. The hare's body twitched and spasmed as the boy and the crone leapt back from the suddenly moving creature. It raised its head and pricked its ears and in a moment was sitting with its haunches tucked under it; sat like a statue, motionless.

The crone had an expression of 'well-I'll-be damned' on her face. The hare walked slowly forward and stared again into the boy's eyes and then curled at his feet in restfulness and closed his eyes and breathed a great sigh and fell into a peaceful sleep.

"What did you say then" said the crone

"I don't know, I, I can't remember now, I don't know where it came from" Boy shook his head as if clearing it after a knock.

"It was his name you said boy, his name, we won't be able to remember it but that's what it was you said, his true animal name. That's a great honour lad, there's not many that ever have the love and luck to utter an animal's true name. You are blessed boy now, you are blessed. 'Twas when I said the name of an animal that I got the knowledge of the plants that I use today. I saved a farmer's horse from dying from the cold and damp one winter's night. I found it stuck in a boggy ditch just before it gave up from exhaustion, I stayed with it reassuring it and tended to it all through the night and as it came in and out of consciousness and stirred for a moment I knew its name, but only once, to call it back and then it was forgotten"

She went on "In the morning I attracted attention with my shouting and they came and saved the horse. If you have ever seen a horse eating along a hedgerow, you'll see they pick and choose the plants they eat like they're right fussy. They know the plants, and they use them as medicine as well as food, adjusting their bodies according to need through eating the different herbs and leaves. 'Twas that knowledge I suddenly gained. Found myself knowing, just knowing which leaf, which herb which bark would do people good"

Lastly she said "You'll find good fortune will favour you in some way now you've known an animal's real name. Something he knows will be in you now."

Breaking from her story she said "But now take him back to your home and keep him warm.

He'll wake in a few hours and then he will go back to the countryside."

"But I was hoping I might keep him as sort of a pet" said the boy, slightly embarrassed knowing the suggestion sounded faintly foolish in his world of practical necessity.

"No lad, there's never good in trying to keep a wild animal for yourself and 'tis known that hares and the like will get fretful and wan and die of heart ache for the freedom of the land that they need. I promise you for his own good you must send him off when he wakes" the crone finished and looked softly at the boy, she knew he didn't really have anything, no mother to love him, a father who meant well but had long since married the drink since losing his wife. If only he had called on the crone he may have been able to save the lass from the fever. The boy, she knew, lived on alone mostly and was a distance from the company of other children in the village. She saw strength and good in him.

The boy looked sad but had lived with the ways of the countryside all his life and knew that was the right thing to do. He picked up a now much healthier feeling Assander whose eyes half opened to recognise him and then shut again. The boy edged to the door.

"Thank you" he said sniffing and raising himself up like the man he longed to be.

"Pleasure" said the crone and straightened a little bit, she had seen many a young boy become fine men in her long life "When fortune favours you, as it will now my lad, you remember the old crone and come see if there is anything I be needing at that time"

"I will" said the boy "I will" and tottered off with his backpack of white furry feet and flopping ears

The crone turned, smiled and went back to her toils.

Chapter 10

Back at home Boy settled the hare into a bed of fresh straw and feeling tired himself lay down beside him.

As dawn broke the boy stirred as was his way. When you have no electric light and no other means of entertainment there is little to do but go to bed when it gets dark and wake when it becomes light.

He heard the waves crashing on the shore and stepped out into a beautiful gentle summer's morning. A far cry from the angry storms of the recent days; such a quick change of weather was typical of the peninsula. He glanced back at the still sleeping hare and decided to make his way to the beach.

He clambered down the steep bank above the beach and made his way over the large stones towards the sand where it met the waves. It was a very low tide so there was plenty of sandy beach. He decided it was a morning for plunging into the waves; his body he knew was none too fresh. In caring for Assander for two nights he had not washed in the stream as usual. The sea water would clean him.

He loved to play in the sea, swimming or, on days like these with the breakers a couple to three feet high, he would just battle against them, dive underneath them or body surf a short distance into the shore.

Taking off his shirt and trousers he waded into the sea; he could not help but take a sharp intake of breath at the first strike of a wave against his bare legs and the spray spattering his thin upper body.

There was nothing for it but to dive in to get over the initial shock. He took a deep breath and plunged forward beneath the next wave. The icy shock made his body feel like it was on fire but it was a fantastic energising feeling.

As he went beneath the water the roar of the surf cut out and he heard the muffled crash of the wave behind him. He swam a few strokes in the space between the incoming waves, savouring the quiet before breaking up into the air, back to the noise of the world above the surface.

The water was white with strands of foam and he was able to lie back in the calm between the swells, his ears under the water back to that more peaceful world. It felt like his body did not end at his limbs but extended into the whole sea, perhaps even the whole universe.

He always felt this way floating in the sea, like the salt water soothed his niggles and vices and irritations. Laying on his back just his face, hands and knees showed above the aqua blue and white water. He stared up at the paling moon in the morning sky, not quite full now and fast fading as the sun came up.

After a short while playing in the surf he made his way back towards the beach, feeling the weight of his limbs return in the land of air and dripping from all parts of his body. His eyes were stinging from the salt water as he looked up the beach. He blinked as a white figure came into focus.

Standing still; it was Assander, staring at him, sitting on his powerful haunches with his feet tucked underneath and his long slender front legs stretching down in front of him. His large ears flicked and turned in different directions constantly. The sea breeze ruffled his pure white pelt.

The boy approached him cautiously, wondering how close this now proud looking being would let him get. Assander's nose twitched and he turned his head slightly to one side as if better to observe the boy with his big blue eye. He was happy to let the boy near him as he trusted him. From the care he knew he had received and the memory of seeing him first when he came back from the meeting with the Moon Goddess he was assured of the boy's nature.

The boy came and chose a large flat rock to sit on near Assander, not chancing alarming him. He was fascinated seeing the hare in his proper stance, so unlike the flaccid, near corpse he had found.

A wave crashed louder than before and Assander flinched and rose on his back legs, front paws hanging down but ready to flee.

"It's alright" Boy said soothingly " 'tis only a wave. I know you must have been frightened, caught in it when it was a storming. It's no place to be in the water when the sea's angry. But on a day like this it can be really good fun. You must have been watching me in the waves you saw they didn't do me no harm."

He eased himself up and gestured towards the water. Without knowing why, Assander started to follow. His trust in the boy just felt right. They walked slowly towards the water's edge, the boy making encouraging noises and holding out his hand as if to pull Assander by an invisible thread. Assander followed with his loping walk, half hopping with his back legs half walking, his haunches high in the air showing the length of his muscular back legs above the large paws.

When they reached the sea shore the waves had subsided and there was just a mirror finish of thin water, a film on the sand. Assander's pads felt chilled on the wet sand. He looked up at the boy who was enthusing and laughing.

A small amount of water came in, no more than half an inch and washed over Assander's paws.

It disorientated him for a moment as he looked down to see the water curling around his legs and the ground distort with the refraction of the water. It made him wobble a bit. Again the boy made soothing noises and Assander decided it was alright.

Then as if from nowhere there was a wave crashing towards them, straight in front of them. Assander did not have time to think to run. The boy, a yard or two ahead of the hare, was whooping with joy as the wave crashed around him. All Assander's instincts could come up with was to jump, so he leapt in the air and right over the wave, clearing it by a good few feet. The boy creased up with laughter as Assander plopped into the shallower water behind the wave and shook himself then looked up with a surprised expression. Just then another wave hit them both side on and knocked them off their feet. Assander writhed and flailed in the water flashing back to the night of the wreck.

The wave spat them both out of its rear as it went on its way up the beach. The boy and Assander sat side by side in the water, Assander looked far less proud and aloof in his now soaked fur, stuck together by the sea water and a piece of sea weed draped over one of his sloping shoulders.

Again the boy laughed and without thinking reached out and hugged the hare to him, laughing and making sounds of joy and calm. Assander felt a bit squashed and ungainly held against the boy's thin chest but he felt the love from the small young body and he knew he was safe. On thinking, he realised he had not been harmed by the water.

In fact, Assander felt elated and for no better reason than pure joy and the closeness with the Universe's energy that this salty foaming water brought, he raced in circles around the boy, water splashing everywhere, then sand, as he spun and skidded around on the exposed sand.

They spent the rest of the morning playing in the surf, Assander leaping over the waves as the boy dived beneath them.

It was late morning as they lay side by side on the beach. The near noon sun, beating down, had dried their bodies leaving salt crusts in the boy's hair and Assander's fur.

"You have to go" said the boy slowly. Assander did not understand the words but felt the change in the boy's energy; the acceptance of before had waned and now there was the feeling of rejection that he knew only too well. He stared at the boy.

"You can't stay with me" said Boy "it isn't right and you must go back to your kind"

The boy stood up and Assander sat and stared up at him, his big ears flat to his back, the skin on his prominent forehead stretched back.

His large eyes stared trying to understand what the boy said. He was muttering something Assander could not understand; it was like a sound heard from underwater for him.

But Assander knew what he meant as he had experienced this before; to be cast out for being different, rejected for nothing more than your accident of birth. There was something in the boy that felt different to Assander though. This did not seem the same rejection through hatred or fear that he had known before. It was as if the boy's body and his inner intent differed.

Assander stared on. How could this other being change from being so caring to being hostile? The boy's eyes seemed to become wet, glassy like the water.

Then he shouted at Assander and lunged forward. The decision was made, aggression had been shown and every nerve ending in the hare's body responded. This was threat, this was what happened in this world, it attacked you, just like the men, the dogs and even his own kind. Animal instinct took over and Assander fled.

He ran across the beach, up the slope, up the steep grassland and beyond the cliffs to gorse and cover. Behind him he heard the boy's voice fading. If he had looked back he would have seen the boy slump to the ground on his knees and hold his head in his hands.

Chapter 11

Assander stopped running some distance along the cliff. He had the sun on his back but did not know where he was going. To his left was the sea, and to his right, grassland and hedges; plenty of familiar features in an unfamiliar land. He spent the afternoon loping along and ate at various points along the hedges, choosing varieties with which he was familiar.

What to do now? He had no knowledge of where his kind might be here. Then again his kind did not want him when he was with them. Nobody seemed to want him.

Up ahead on the cliff's edge he saw some white creatures in the distance. He was the only pure white animal he had ever seen apart from some of the sheep back in Ireland after the rain but even they were not as white as him.

These things on the edge of the cliff edge were white, brilliant white. He started to run, not his full speed but a quick run towards these other white beings. Perhaps they would accept him as being of their colour.

As he neared the white creatures he recognised them as birds and slowed but by then they had already seen him and took off in a flurry of beating wings and the most awful screeching. Screeching like he had never known before. It disorientated him and then there seemed to be wings and beaks and feathers everywhere.

I am of your colour he said *I too am white do you not see?*

The replies came in a cacophony of messages in his brain from a myriad of sources

White you may be but we know not your kind ... ...animals of the ground steal our eggs ... ...and our young...   ...You may be white but we see you for what you are...   ...Reynard he is Reynard   ...whatever disguise you might think you have taken you do not fool us....

And with that the gulls started to attack him pecking and jabbing; flying, swooping, nipping his ears, pulling his fur, knocking him sideways. It was no good he had to run again and this time he took flight at his top speed. The gulls chased but his turns and twists confused them and they crashed into each other and flew in the wrong direction.

He ran back down the cliff side, leaping from mound to mound and headed inland as he went; down into a valley, over a stream darting from rock to rock and up the other side towards more gorse and cover. He broke out of the cover on the next cliff top and slowed in an open field. To his left he could see a church tower and in the distance houses, to his right was just sea. Up ahead was a stone building and as the afternoon was starting to fade he thought he might be able to shelter there.

When he reached the stone building he found it had no front or back just sides. No roof. It was adequate for him to shelter from the wind that had now licked up and he nestled into a corner.

He sighed and felt so purposeless. After the joy of the morning with the boy and a feeling of love he had not known since he had been with his mother the rejection from the child and then the gulls left him feeling as dejected and sad as he had ever felt.

And then it rained ... and with no roof he was once again soaked to the skin. He shivered and whimpered slightly.

Chapter 12

Assander huddled in the old ruin, cold and sad, he felt rejected and dejected. It seemed he would never be accepted or find his place. As for the Goddess's talk of his gift it seemed running was all he could do and it was just as well he was good at that.

He drifted in and out of a shallow sleep dreaming only of chases and threats seen and unseen. In his private dream-world he was not aware that the rain had stopped and the moon had risen and was now over the cliff top on which he had chosen this night's resting place.

If he had been more awake he would also have noticed a large splendid white stag that had made its way towards the same cliff top. It stood still proudly holding its head and surveying the calm sea with the silvery moonlight glittering on the rippling waves. He breathed the cool briny air that came in over the water and listened to the soft waves breaking far below.

Had Assander been awake he would have seen the stag look up at the moon and gaze, rapt, for what could have been a moment or an hour. It seemed the whole night went silent as if the world, maybe even the universe, had stopped and nobody had noticed. The stag, with its fine antlers and raised head silhouetted against the bright full moon, seemed to nod and then look towards the ruin.

As with all animals' movement on soft ground with none of the noise made by the clothes of humankind they can arrive without sound. Assander was staring at the broken shards of rock on the floor of the ruin, his back to the large arch that faced inland. He leapt from the ground as he felt hot breath on his ears and looking round saw a huge wet white snout looming towards him. He jumped into the opposite corner of the ruin. The huge head of the stag was peering around the edge of the archway. Assander was sitting back on his hind legs with his front paws gathered up towards his chest and stomach, his ears pricked up to full height.

That is a splendid pair of ears you have young man. Good for hearing no doubt, but I wonder how they are at listening came the deep resonant contact from the stag.

Assander had never seen such a big deer before; the deer in his native Ireland were much smaller and brown... brown! This deer, unless it was a trick of the moonlight, was white. Like him!

You're white, said Assander rather unnecessarily

Yes? answered the stag rather nonplussed by the statement of the obvious, *Welcome to Hartland, you have obviously come a long way. I am sorry your first impressions have been not entirely kindly*

No they haven't said Assander feeling instantly comfortable in the company of this large animal. It had a calm and steady demeanour and energy that emanated acceptance

Come with me said the stag *you can be safe here if you know where you should be*

Assander and the stag walked off together and, deep in conversation, slowly wandered back down the hill towards a wooded valley with the lights of a large country house visible at its far end in the distance.

~~~

Assander spent the next few weeks with the stag, wandering the woodlands of the peninsula.

The stag listened to Assander's story and told him many things. It seemed from the knowledge the stag showed that he must have been here then and now. Often some of the other animals would gather and listen to the stag talking to Assander. He asked one squirrel if the stag had always been, and he said he knew no creature that did not remember him always being here. He said he knew that a human name for a male deer can be a 'hart' and that the land in which they lived was called Hartland by the men who lived here.

Have you always been here? Assander asked the stag one day

The stag answered *Well I have been here all my life, then and now, which to a young one like you would seem like forever. It has been my kind, and those from which I come, that have always lived here and they taught me what I tell you. And I tell you Assander you are special, different from those to which you were born, not better just with a special gift.*

Assander told the stag of his meeting with the Goddess but that he knew not what gift he might have, what talent she referred to that he should use or risk losing it to the universe never to be found again for aeons.

Then we shall talk and find your talent decreed the stag

~~~

And as the days went past Assander told of his disappointment and bitterness in the rejection he had experienced. The stag understood but helped Assander see some of the reasons why, through misunderstanding, those who are different can cause suspicion and even fear in those who do not understand them.

Assander told of his time with the boy and was angry and hurt at the boy's sudden rejection. Surely from his first caring and attention he knew Assander meant no harm. The stag explained the boy's action saying how wild animals cannot live in the world of man, captive and constrained, and so the boy, having been brought up to appreciate and know about animals, had done the right thing to send Assander away. And so Assander understood a bit more.

The stag explained that hares are solitary creatures and mostly live alone except when coming together in their rings for mating time. He told him also of the many times hares feature in the teachings and history of man. Hartland had long been a place where learned men and women; writers, historians and artists had come to spend time and help themselves understand.

These too were solitary types, it was necessary for them to be alone to fulfil their purpose to write and create; they needed the space for their thoughts to arrange and their stories to be formed. The stag and his forefathers had found they could listen to the pictures in the heads of these solitary souls who sat and made marks on paper and the deer understood their thoughts.

The stag told him one day *Once, then, there was a man who came from across the mighty water we look out onto. He looked different from the other men who live here. He had dark skin and long black hair and wore coloured glass in strands around his neck. He would walk in the woodlands of the peninsula and sit in the clearings for hours, totally still, whilst we animals could come up to him. Some of the squirrels and birds even took to climbing and sitting on him.*

Assander listened fascinated by such a story of a man so close to the animals. It reminded Assander of his time with Boy.

The stag went on *The pictures in his head were so many, they were very clear. We could see his kind, they knew themselves as Algonquin. In their then the great creator spirit was a hare called Glooskap. He was lauded for having tricked the giant who brought winter by imprisoning the summer. He persuaded him into talking and telling stories for so long that the fire at which they sat went out and the very frost the giant used to imprison summer froze the giant and Glooskap. Glooskap awoke before the giant and was able to bring summer back to their land.*

Assander listened in awe; a great hare spirit and a man whose thoughts could be heard like an animal's.

And so the days wore on peacefully and slowly as Assander learnt more of hares and their connection with the spirits of nature and the renewal of the seasons. The stag told him of how each being contributes to the onward circle of life as death gives way to birth in a constant cycle. Through our actions or our genes or both we become part of the progression of life; The Great Progress.

The stag explained that as we are absorbed back into the universe on death we become part of everything again. Our consciousness may be born again but without the memory of the being we were before. This is why, when we are given form, we must use the gifts or talents we have, to do for others what we can. In doing so, those talents will inspire actions in others and our contribution towards the Great Progress will live on beyond our time. If not those gifts will be lost and may not be granted again for aeons.

Chapter 13

And Assander sat listening and learning, still wondering to what the goddess Cynthia might have been referring for his talent. The stag was in no hurry to try to find the talent, understanding that it was for Assander to know.

One day Assander told the stag of his experience when the storms had hit the boat and when he had been with the boy.

Ah... nodded the Stag *After you arrived I heard the men in the fields tell of the stories being told in the tavern on the Quay. The crew of the wrecked ship told of a white ghost that had twitched and writhed and brought the storm that wrecked them*

No, no, said Assander *I did not cause the storm, it is the storm that causes such great pain in me.*

It feels like my head has a great weight on it and that thorns pierce my skull through to the backs of my eyes. I feel this even before anyone hears the storm. Assander was distressed

The great white hart spoke *Calm yourself little one, this is not a curse this is just your sensitivity to the ways of our mother nature. I remember then there was a poet called Cowper that came to the peninsula to write his beautiful verse, and he had two pet hares. He would recount the story that they both became fractious and then excited at the drawing near of a thunderstorm and would prance and dance around when the storm hit. Perhaps like them you can learn to feel the storm for its pure energy, not as a threat or danger to you. To watch the storms from the Point fighting and crashing out at sea can be an inspiring and wonderful sight*

Not so wonderful if you are in a boat in such a clash of storms said Assander

Maybe this is your gift Assander, I don't know how or why but maybe it is finished the stag

~~~

So it was that a few days later as the hare and the stag walked by a stream late in the afternoon Assander felt the pressure on his head that foretold him of a storm. The stag noticed Assander's left eye flicker and his head twitch as if a thorn might have been pushed into him.

What is it Assander? asked the stag

I feel it Assander winced against the pain *there is a storm coming, a big one, a mighty one. It travels fast across the sea from where I came from*

But the skies are clear Assander; the air is sweet and calm. There is no sign of cloud and certainly not of a storm said the stag

Assander answered *I tell you I feel a storm coming and soon* and with that his legs weakened and he almost fell to the ground. His head lowered and his great ears fell forward as his legs struggled to keep him upright

The stag spoke *If what you say is true and there is a great storm at sea then the fishing fleet from Hartland Quay are in great danger. They are due out tonight, all of them; it is the start of the season for the silver mackerel and I heard them boasting of how they would all fill their nets to bursting on the sea's harvest expected this year. If they all go out and are lost in the storm, all of our mankind in Hartland will suffer for the loss of the menfolk. Assander you must go to the Quay to warn them.*

But how? pleaded Assander

The stag answered *I don't know, that is up to you, you know that running helps your mind to clear. Run now, as fast as you can, to the fishermen at the Quay and do something to stop them going out on their fishing trip.* And with that he moved his great antlers towards the Quay encouraging Assander to move

So having learnt to trust the great knowledge and experience of the stag Assander took him at his word and set off at full speed to the Quay.

Chapter 14

Assander's mighty back legs pounded the ground and as the energy coursed through his body it helped to drive back the thorn-pain that pushed into his temples. Without thought he passed the ruin in a blur and ran down the winding roadway that leads to the Quay. He glanced left and right at the mighty cliffs that rose up above the cove in which the little fishing fleet was moored.

He ran between buildings towards the slipway where the fishermen had gathered to prepare for their fishing trip. They were all on board, either head down arranging nets and lines, or preparing to cast off; they didn't notice his arrival. He paused and then ran along the quay wall and down onto the level in front of the ropes mooring the boats. He sat for a moment and looked at the men from the quayside, sitting back on his haunches and raising his back up and his ears up to full extension. His head quivered from side to side as he felt the storm's energy in his body.

For a moment nothing happened and then one fisherman glanced up.

"Well I'll be....a white rabbit...what are they putting in the ale around here?" he cried in his coarse voice

One of the men from the smugglers' vessel was working alongside and looked up, his eyes widened

"That's no rabbit that's the ghost we had on our boat the one that came with the storm!" he shouted

"Its a hare!" said the other "A white hare"

"It'll be hair-less when I geddit!" cursed the other

And with that they both jumped off the boat towards Assander, the others shouted and encouraged them. Assander shot right then left, between some legs, round some others, up onto the edge of a boat then back on the quay, round and around as the fishermen jumped from their boats. They chased and swatted with hooks, staffs and rods, makeshift weapons swiftly gathered from their boats.

Then he made a break for it up the slipway and back towards the tavern and cottages. The gap between the two buildings was filling with drinkers from the bar as they spilled out to find out what the commotion was all about. They spread across the gap as Assander ran towards them.

He was going at full speed as he reached them weaving as he went. The first man bent down to grasp at thin air as he went through his legs; the next made for a rugby tackle but missed him too, the third and fourth were behind a table and moved to cover all exits. Assander ran up the bench onto the table and in a great leap jumped over the heads of the men that stood between him and the route up out from the quay.

Although a great steep slope, Assander's and the men's blood was pumping so fast they were able to run upwards without much effort. The rabble followed him with staffs and hooks in their hands, baying for his blood. As they reached the top some of the men who perhaps spent more time in the bar at the tavern than on the fishing boats were wheezing and puffing, but the fittest kept going.

Assander turned at the top and ran out onto the cliff top. He could still feel the storm, greater now pressing down. But his concern was more with the band of men-hounds following behind him. He saw the ruin ahead that had housed him on that first night when he had met the stag. It did not really afford any shelter but it was the only real cover on the top of this cliff.

He ran and ran, weakened by the storm pushing the pain into his head. As he reached the ruin he swerved to turn into the side facing the sea and to his surprise there was Boy inside standing there. He leapt towards him and into his arms, knocking him over and back onto the rough floor.

He stood on Boy's chest and looked down with his big blue eyes into those of the young lad. Assander's chest was heaving and panting with the effort of the run and with the pain of the storm portent. Then he writhed, flinched and spasmed as he had done the night the boy had looked after him. He collapsed into Boy's arms twitching.

The men arrived at the ruin and gathered at the opening panting and coughing.

The first man said "Put it down boy, whatever it is it t'ain't no good"

"It's a hare, I know him I rescued him, I found him on the beach the morning after the last wreck. I know what he's doing. I saw it before, he got like this when there was a storm brewing, a thunderstorm" cried the boy

"T'ain't no storm now boy, we's off out for the biggest haul of fish this season" scoffed one of the men.

But what with all the commotion and the chase, the fishermen had not seen the dark clouds scudding from the horizon across the sea into the clear blue sky. They now stood, soon to be caught up in a maelstrom of wind and rain that would whip the sea into a frenzy like none had ever known.

There was a distant low rumble of thunder like a deep warning to the heart of every fisherman and a fork of lightening flashed across the sky and down to the sea, accompanied by a sound that felt like the sky itself might have split.

"Well I'll be" said the one of the fishermen

"See" said the boy "he knew, he knows when there is going to be a storm, it makes him act all funny like he's ill. He came to warn you"

"Tis true, he was behavin' like that on our boat. If we hadn't have been chasin' him we'd have set off just now an' be in that storm" said the smuggler "I think he just saved our lives"

Assander stretched himself up in the boy's arms and once again their eyes met in a knowing stare.

 The boy said softly "Thank you Assander", and the hare leapt from his arms and at full speed fled towards the wooded valleys beyond the cliff tops.

"Come on boy" said the first fishermen "Come on lads let's be getting on back afore this storm breaks here, I think there's a few pints with our names on 'em!"

The men cheered and slapped each other's backs. As they wandered back more slowly towards the tavern, they watched the storm racing towards them with its lightening flashes and wall of rain and thanked their lucky stars... or maybe the hare, that they hadn't taken their boats out that evening.

"What did ya call him?" asked the smuggler to the boy

"I don't remember" answered the boy honestly

"What do you want to be when you grows up boy?" said the fishermen

"A skipper of a fishing boat like you sir" said the boy looking up

"Well" said the fishermen rubbing the top of the boy's head and tousling his hair "We'll see what we can be doin' about that. Come and see me tomorrow and you can help get the boat ready"

As they sat in the bar the storm reached land and they turned their collars to the rain-lashed window and drank a toast to the White Hare of Hartland.

Chapter 15

Assander made his way back through the woods to seek out the white hart. When he found him the wise old stag already knew of Assander's exploits.

They will be forever grateful for your saving of their fleet. I believe you may have found your talent Assander said the stag

You mean to tell if a storm is coming could be of help to humankind. You mean that is my talent? asked Assander slightly surprised

It is a rare one young man. To be able to impart knowledge useful to the safety of men will make you invaluable. Not only will you be safe from hunters here, you will be able to guide the

fishermen and the hunters across the rest of this land will accept you too explained the stag

My talent....my home whispered Assander.

He fell silent and nodded slowly feeling comfortable at last.

~~~

And so Assander lived on the peninsula. And his gift was spoken of through all the animals. And come the following spring the ring of hares at Stoke invited him to join them and Assander found himself the subject of much interest amongst the young does.

To have children that might be like Assander in looks and gift would mean the hunters would leave them alone and the fisherfolk would value them. Assander boxed and played and took great joy in the good spirit and friendship that a ring of hares should share when all are looking for the attention of a mate.

~~~

And as the seasons pass there is always an Assander to help the fisherfolk of the ports of the south west, running along harbour walls or between the boats pulled up on the shore, a sign that the sea will be too angry for them that day. The Assanders of *now* are the same as the original one *then,* his offspring for the generations after him inheriting the look that had set him apart once then but now was prized. With his looks came the knowledge of sea storms and the benefit that was bestowed on those that knew what it meant. Seeing the white hare in a fishing port meant the hunters would leave it alone, happy to forego their game to secure fish for a future supper.

~~~

And what about Boy? Oh, he turned up for work that summer's morning and never looked back. He was a hard worker and the captain was pleased to have him as crew. But there was more to his skill than muscle; as he crewed more it became apparent that the boy seemed to have a gift for knowing where the best fishing would be, almost like he could hear the fish.

And the boy grew into a fine man and became one of the most respected captains on the coast; skilful in his fishing, knowing instinctively where to find the best catch but also feeling how much to take of a shoal to preserve the stocks for all time. And he was a fair man with time for all, especially those who were different and misunderstood. He would give them shelter or food if they needed it where others would shun them for their difference. Time and again the ones he helped would return with payment of some kind as their own success grew when they found their place in the world.

~~~

And the old crone? Well, a certain well-respected fishing captain saw to it that she never wanted for fresh fish and firewood, and would have no-one speak ill of her in his company, and her reputation spread and her life was comfortable.

Chapter 16

The harbour at Hartland Quay was destroyed by a great storm in the late 19th century. But of course the fishing fleet were not at sea; they had seen Assander on the shoreline that afternoon, their boats were therefore securely moored.

They were all in the tavern listening to the wind howl outside. After the little port was destroyed they had to move to a different harbour but they had their vessels and their lives.

~~~

And if you spend a long evening enjoying the company and hospitality at a tavern in Hartland and for want of a lift or for the joy of a stroll on a clear night, with the millions of stars that present their show over the cliffs, you might

find yourself walking home on the cliff top ...
perhaps a little unsteadily but happy.

It is said that if you have a clear and generous
heart then if you look across to the old ruin you
might be lucky enough to see the silhouettes of
a large proud stag standing next to a seated hare
looking out to sea, apparently deep in
conversation... although you won't hear a
thing...

 ...and you will maybe think it a trick of that
silvery moonlight or maybe you will smile
because you know who they are... either which
way you won't remember in the morning what
you saw. You will know you saw something but
you won't be able to recall what...

... and you will laugh at your mislaid memory,
and blame the ale you had *then*, and go on with
your day feeling a bit better *now* than you did,
but not knowing why.